PEANUTS®
Lose the Blanket, LINUS!

By Charles M. Schulz
Adapted by Tina Gallo
Illustrated by Robert Pope

SIMON SPOTLIGHT
New York London Toronto Sydney New Delhi

SIMON SPOTLIGHT

An imprint of Simon & Schuster Children's Publishing Division
1230 Avenue of the Americas, New York, New York 10020
First Simon Spotlight paperback edition October 2015
SIMON SPOTLIGHT and colophon are registered trademarks of Simon & Schuster, Inc.
For information about special discounts for bulk purchases, please contact Simon & Schuster
Special Sales at 1-866-506-1949 or business@simonandschuster.com.
Manufactured in the United States of America 0815 LAK
10 9 8 7 6 5 4 3 2 1
ISBN 978-1-4814-4129-2
ISBN 978-1-4814-4130-8 (eBook)

This is Linus. Linus loves his blanket more than anything in the world.

His blanket is soft. It makes him feel happy. He likes the way the fabric feels against his cheek. It makes him feel calm. When Linus holds his blanket, he feels like everything will be all right, no matter what happens.

His sister, Lucy, however, thinks differently. His blanket annoys her. "When are you going to get rid of that silly blanket?" she asks.

"It's not silly," Linus replies. "It makes me feel happy. Maybe if you had a blanket, you wouldn't be so crabby."

"Crabby? Who's crabby?" Lucy shouts.

I guess from now on I'll keep my suggestions to myself, Linus thinks.

"THIS IS IT!" Lucy shouts. Her voice startles Linus, and he jumps. Lucy grabs his blanket and runs off.

I wonder what that was all about, Linus thinks. He shrugs and turns to pick up his blanket. But his blanket is nowhere to be found!

Linus is still frantically searching for his blanket when Lucy returns. She has a huge grin on her face.
"I buried your blanket!" she tells him.

Linus can't believe his ears.

"You *buried* my blanket?" he yells. "You can't do that! I'll die without that blanket! I'll be like a fish out of water! I'll die! I'll die!"

Lucy just stares at Linus. She doesn't say a word.

Linus gets very angry. "Tell me where you buried it!" he demands.

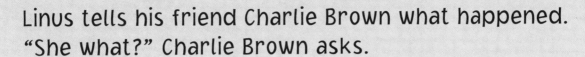

Linus tells his friend Charlie Brown what happened.
"She what?" Charlie Brown asks.
"She buried my blanket, Charlie Brown!" Linus cries.
"She said she was going to cure me of the habit once
and for all, so she buried my blanket!"
Linus looks around at his huge backyard. "How am I
ever going to find it?" he says.

Charlie Brown decides to sleep over at Linus's house to help him get through the first night without his blanket. He pulls up a chair and watches Linus as he sleeps.

"Ohhhh . . . ," Linus moans. He tosses and turns in his sleep.

This is going to be a long night, Charlie Brown thinks.

Suddenly Linus opens his eyes. He looks at Charlie Brown hopefully. "Is it morning yet?" he asks.

"No, it's only ten o'clock," Charlie Brown replies.

"Ten o'clock?!" Linus exclaims. This night is going to last forever!" He lets out a long sigh. "Anyway, Charlie Brown, it's nice of you to sit up with me this first night."

Charlie Brown smiles at Linus. "This is what friends are for," he says.

"Good old Charlie Brown!" Linus says.

A little while later, Linus closes his eyes again. *Ah, that's good,* Charlie Brown thinks. *He's finally gone to sleep. Maybe if he makes it through the night without his blanket, he'll be all right. Sleep is just what he needs.*

"WELL, HOW'S HE DOING?" Lucy's voice booms through the bedroom as she stomps in to check on Linus.

"So much for a good night's rest," Charlie Brown says with a sigh.

The next day Lucy comes over to chat with Charlie Brown.

"You think I'm being mean because I buried Linus's blanket, don't you?" she asks.

Charlie Brown doesn't say anything.

"Well, I'm not!" Lucy continues. "I'm really doing him a favor! He's too weak to ever break the habit by himself. He's as weak as . . . why, he's as weak as *you* are, Charlie Brown!"

I don't think I like that comparison, Charlie Brown thinks.

Charlie Brown tries everything he can think of to help his friend. "I have a suggestion, Linus," he says. "Why don't you let me try to give you a substitute? Would you like this dish towel?"

Linus does not like that idea at all. "Would you give a starving dog a rubber bone?" he asks. "No thank you!"

Charlie Brown shrugs. "I'm out of ideas," he says.

From the moment Linus wakes up the next day, he feels terrible. He goes into the kitchen and takes out a box of cereal for breakfast. He pours some milk on the flakes and takes a bite. He pushes the bowl away. *I can't even eat . . . everything tastes sour,* he thinks.

Lucy, meanwhile, feels just fine. She is relaxing, reading a book. "Please tell me where you buried it," Linus begs.

Lucy doesn't answer.

"I've just got to find that blanket, Charlie Brown," Linus says. "Lucy won't tell me where she buried it, so I've got to dig until I find it." Linus shovels as he speaks.

Charlie Brown admires Linus's determination. "Good luck!" he calls after him.

Linus keeps digging. "Got to find it! Got to find it!" he says to himself. "Got to dig everywhere until I find that blanket! Got to find it! Got to find it!" Linus says.

"Got to find it!" Linus repeats as he continues on his way.

Snoopy can't understand why Linus is so upset. Finding things that are buried is easy for Snoopy! He sniffs around a little bit . . . and there it is!

"MY BLANKET!" Linus yells. "Oh, Snoopy! You found it! You found it! You found it!" Linus says over and over again.

When Linus finally lets him go, Snoopy promptly goes back to his doghouse. *I've done my good deed for the day,* he thinks. *Time for a nap!*

The next day Charlie Brown talks to Lucy about Linus and his blanket. "I hear Linus got his blanket back," Charlie Brown says.

Lucy frowns. "Yeah, your nosy dog found it and dug it up," she says. "Oh well. I don't care anymore. I'm through trying to help people. They never appreciate it, anyway."

"NOSY DOG!" she shouts.

"Hee hee!" Snoopy giggles. He isn't the least bit sorry he helped Linus get his blanket back!

Linus can't stop hugging his blanket. "My blanket! I got it back! I can't believe it! My good old blanket!" Linus says.

He holds it out in front of him and studies it. "It's been buried beneath the ground for days and days," he says. "It's dirty, it's ragged, it's torn, and it's even a little moldy."

Then he hugs it again. "But it's *my* blanket!" he says with a happy sigh.

"You do realize you can't hold on to your blanket forever," Lucy says. "Someday you are going to have to lose the blanket, Linus, whether you like it or not."

Linus tries to imagine being a grown-up. He pictures going to work in a suit and a tie. He knows he probably can't bring his blanket to work with him.

Linus nods. "That's very true, Lucy," he says. "I realize *someday* I'll have to give up my blanket."

He grins at Lucy. "But not today!"
Lucy rolls her eyes. "I give up!" she says.